Zombies and Papercuts

Ima Ghoul

The Written Word Publishing

First Published 2024

ISBN   978-0-9756532-4-1 (Print) 978-1-7643944-0-6 (ebook)

Publisher: The Written Word Publishing

Cover: designed by YD La Mar

Contents

Chapter One

Typical Saturday louts

The steady, rhythmic tick of the large clock above the checkout desk of the small library dulls my senses. I remove the book from the trolley and file it according to author and genre in front of me, unaware of civilisation's impending and hilarious doom creeping towards me.

Let me introduce myself, my name is Alara and I am a librarian in a small country town in South Australia and a local nobody. Constantly the butt of everyone's joke, I would win the award for the 'most belittled teen' in high school. Back then, I cloistered myself among wood and tome, my bitter tears running down my face then my hands and on to crisp white paper. That new book smell always brought me comfort, its contents filled with glamour, adventure and extraordinary friendship, all the things that were lacking in my own life.

Would you believe it, I am thirty-three and have never been pashed? For you, who are unaware of Australian slang, this refers to a passionate kiss.

I sigh, the trolley's wheels screech with protest on the faded carpet as I wheel it behind the desk. I sit down and begin placing the matching cards in the back of returned books, ready to be reshelved. I glance sidelong at the calendar, October 31st, 1981, and smile to myself. Today is my birthday and I have promised myself an incredible dinner and I am looking forward to it.

I stand with a load of books in my hand and smile down at a few familiar titles that have given me great comfort, from tales of beings tossing evil rings into volcanoes and overcoming adversity with the aid of loyal friends, to ravens saying very little in eerie poems intended to scare the wit from you, to more mundane sources such as encyclopedias, survival guides and dictionaries. Books are an incredible testament to the wit and imagination of the human brain, and I am glad to have filled mine with their knowledge.

After placing the books down on the "to be shelved" trolley, I finger my keys absentmindedly in the pocket of my jeans and lean down to grab my handbag.

'Grrrrrr.'

I stiffen, unsure of what that noise could possibly be, and straighten up, forgetting my bag.

'Urrgh.'

My hands shake and I glance around, looking for something to defend myself with, and turn to face the double doors. I blink in surprise; one door is open and slams against the wall as if a huge gust of paranormal wind has forced it open. I let out a hollow laugh, trying to still my nerves.

'Unng.'

The hairs on the back of my neck prickle like a cat ready to pounce and I turn on my heel, the open door to my back. A figure in a tan trench coat, a shield against the still sometimes chilly spring nights, runs their hand down the spine of the encyclopedia. I gulp, fear slicing through me as if those hands had stroked my own back. The streaks of red dripping from calloused hands blends pleasantly with the maroon-backed tomes.

'Can I help you?' I manage to squeeze out as my mouth is suddenly dry.

'Errr,' says the figure.

I roll my eyes assuming this person has stumbled across from the local pub. Being a Saturday evening, we do get the occasional drinker coming in near closing, stumbling around and asking why they are here rather than in their own homes.

'Excuse me, we are closing. If you follow me, I can show you out.' I shake myself, realising the person is bleeding and take a step towards them. 'Excuse me, do you need assistance?'

The figure turns and I stumble back towards a nearby shelf. The man's face is a horrible shade of vomit green; his eyes bulge and fixate on me as he licks his lips.

'Sir, are you okay?' I scramble up against the bookshelf, grab the nearest thing and glance at the title. 'The Ghouls Came Knocking,' I mutter.

I take a shuddering breath as the man suddenly shambles towards me, his hands outstretched as if to choke me. I need to get away and seek help. I wince and groan as I toss the precious book, followed by others, reading each title to ascertain if they should be freed from destruction.

The Guide to Sunday Walks. I toss it and it slaps the man's face. He stops suddenly as the book slides down his face. My eyes follow the book as it thuds to the floor. The man's coat gapes open, revealing his horrific injuries. The skin is peeling away to reveal bone and a green sludge drips from a huge bite wound in the centre of his chest. I cover my nose as the smell of decay wafts towards me.

Dellen's Guide to Romance. I hurl this book and it connects with the man's wound. The man whimpers and cocks his head. 'Oooowwww.'

A scream boils up from inside, threatening to overwhelm me. 'What do you want?'

'Br . . . Brains.'

'Are you a zombie?' I ask.

The man raises a brow and laughs, a strange low growl and half laugh. 'What are you, a book short of a library?'

'Plenty here.' I toss another book at the man, zombie, or whatever he is. 'Zombies don't talk so well.'

'How many zombies have you met?' The man suddenly launches himself at me. 'Now let me glean that knowledge from your tasty brain.'

I run, slamming into the shelf behind me. The man's large body collides with mine. There is a creak as the shelves topple forward. The man's bulging eyes widen as a pile of books crashes into him. I dive out of the way, but not before I reach back and retrieve my keys that had fallen out of my pocket, like some great researcher reaching for an errant hat. Crash, the shelf pins the man to the ground.

I hover over him and he groans. 'While you're under there read a book, there's more knowledge here than you'll ever need.'

Triumphant, I bolt towards the door. Outside, the local populace shambles haphazardly over crossing, road and footpath, mumbling to themselves about how tasty brains are.

Chapter Two

Cricket, the hero's game.

I try to be as inconspicuous as possible. The night is suddenly chilly and I shiver, drawing my lightweight jacket around me, covering my blue t-shirt. My name badge perched across my chest captures the sudden light as the streetlights flicker on. I lower my head and shuffle forwards. I just need to get to my car and home. I turn my head and sigh as I stare at the pub where I would have had my evening repast.

A woman stops in front of me, hunched over and panting. I halt and wait. My car is parked across the road. The only set of traffic lights change from red to green. My mouth is agape as cars slowly move forward, swerving across the road and gently colliding into a car on the opposite side. A car door opens and a man sprints towards me, his mouth set in a grim frown, his white tank top smeared with blood, a cricket bat in hand.

'Four!' he cries as the lady in front turns and runs towards me, her perm dishevelled, her perfectly manicured nails now chipped.

'Stop, Irene,' I yell, recognising my neighbour.

As the stranger swings his bat, I scream, the noise alerting the others around me. Growls and slurred words greet me as Irene's head is knocked clean off her body and lands straight in my hands. I stare at her green face, the bulging eyes blinking with recognition as she smiles. 'Hello, Alara love.'

I drop the head, my body trembling. I clench my legs together as my bladder becomes my enemy threatening to release its contents. A hand covers my mouth; the heat of another body suddenly pressed up behind me.

'Strewth, be quiet or these drongos will chew you to bits.' The man behind me suddenly grabs my arm and sprints to the car in front of me. 'Get in,' he hollers as I am pulled along.

'I don't ride with strangers,' I mutter.

The man shrugs, releases my hand and hurries around to the driver's side, hopping in and closing the door. 'Suit yourself.'

A collective growl shatters the preternatural quiet, and the sound of thongs slapping bitumen spurs me forward as I climb into the car, slamming the door as twenty zombie sheilas and blokes rush us. My saviour plants his foot down and the Holden Commodore accelerates rapidly. I turn in my seat, glancing out the back window as the stranger's gallant steed whisks us away to safety.

'Hello, Alara, I am Gavin,' says my rescuer.

'How did—'

Gavin laughs heartily and tilts his head to my name badge. 'So, you're a librarian.'

I nod and his attention returns to the road. 'I'm a local farmer. Cattle mainly. Nothing better than a steak.'

He licks his lips and my body begins to shake uncontrollably. 'You aren't—'

My new acquaintance slows the vehicle then pulls over and puts it in park. He leans across and pats my hand. 'I'm not a zombie, okay.' His eyes soften and I realise he is handsome in an Australian workhorse kind of way: big calloused hands, strong jaw, kind eyes and sandy blonde hair styled in a mullet. 'You look like you're about to chunder.'

I scramble out of the car as I hastily throw open the door. Rushing away from the vehicle, I empty my guts. I turn my back to a tree trunk and slide down its surface, avoiding the bush I vomited into, and hug my knees to my chest. Hot tears slide down my cheeks and my breath quickens. Zombies. How is that possible? 'Zombies are real!' I cry.

Gavin approaches me and leans down. 'Where do you live, love? I'll drop you off.'

'Did you really knock someone's block off with a cricket bat?' I ask, the question almost shuddering out of my body.

'Did you know them?' asks Gavin.

I nod. 'My neighbour.'

'Ah, so you live next to old Irene.' Gavin stands and stretches, the palms of his hands on the back of his head, arms bent at the elbow. 'I'm sorry to bother you, but we best get going.'

I stand and look around. We are on the outskirts of my little town. The red soil now dark shadows under a star-filled sky. Slightly green salt bush blanketing the dry soil almost invisible due to a lack of light.

I raise my eyes to the servo in front of me. Three petrol bowsers near an ancient building; the white paint peeling under the scrutiny of the streetlights. I smile as my eyes alight on the glass phone box; dirt streaks the panels. The black coin-operated rotary phone encased within beckons to me of services that will rush to my aid if I just call.

'I think we should call the police,' I offer.

Gavin shrugs. 'Can't hurt.'

I try to remain quiet. My heels click on the road, the sound almost taboo in the deadly silence. A cold wind plays cheekily at the tendrils of my strawberry blonde hair as I pull open the glass doors and step up into the cement-floored booth. It smells faintly of cigarettes and ammonia. I reach for my handbag. Bloody heck, I left it behind.

Gavin knocks on the open glass door and I turn. He shoves his large mass inside the tight space. His warmth presses against my back as he reaches into his pocket and removes some coins. The coins clatter as they are pushed into the coin slot. I gulp, nervous at his nearness, and raise the receiver to my ear, flicking the dial towards the appropriate numbers and relief floods through me as the line connects.

Gavin leans closer as I speak. 'Hello.'

'Grrrr,' the recipient on the other end says.

'Umm . . . we need help, something strange is going on,' I spit out.

There are some horrible crunching and squelching noises before I shiver as the voice continues. 'Brains.'

A warm hand clasps mine before lifting the receiver and replacing it back in the cradle.

'I don't think the coppers will be much help.' Gavin winks and I feel my insides turn to jelly, but not out of fear.

'Your place is a few moments from here so we best get a move on.' The man pressed against my back draws away and hurries to his car.

I take a deep breath, trying to encourage the heat in my cheeks to dissipate, and follow. As we drive towards my house, Gavin turns to me. 'I live at the big farm about twenty minutes away. You're welcome to stay there.'

I shake my head as the car pulls up in my driveway, the engine now idling as the car is put in park. I leave the safety of the vehicle and smile. 'Thank you for helping me,' I mutter lowering my eyes as my natural shyness creeps in.

Gavin grins. 'Think nothing of it.' He pulls a pen from the glovebox and scrawls on a bit of paper torn from an old classic novel. 'Here's my number.'

'Thanks,' I mumble as I snatch the piece of paper and sprint towards the door, hand plunging into my pocket. I settle my shaking hand as I force the key into the lock and push the door open. As the car reverses out the driveway, I hurry inside and slam the door shut.

Chapter Three

Yeast on rye and my plumbing

That's when the gravity of the situation fully encompasses me. This could be the end of the world like all those survivalists predicted, and I am woefully unprepared. I rush through my hallway, glancing into the master bedroom, then the bathroom, toilet and final bedroom, before I enter the large lounge room equipped with cheery hearth, bookshelves and two comfy armchairs. Phew, no danger yet.

I hurry to the kitchen and pull open my lime green refrigerator and stare at my staples: a few apples, condiments, a loaf of bread, bung fritz, eggs, butter and milk. Enough for a day or two. I turn towards the sink and throw open the overhead lemon-coloured cupboard and shove the few cans around: baked beans, a jar of half-eaten vegemite, salt, pepper, a couple of bags of chips, sugar, tea and coffee. I can do this. I can stay inside until the authorities get it sorted. That's as good a plan as any and this is unlikely an apocalypse. I smile to myself and kick off my shoes, wriggling my toes on the green and grey chequered linoleum.

Filling the kettle at the sink, I plug it into the wall and, with a click and a rush, the kettle begins to heat and boil. As I wait, I place a teabag in the cup along with some sugar. I don't normally take it with sugar but today I'm feeling a little wild. I pour the water in and sigh as the tea begins to steep; the smell reaches my nostrils, comforting. I pour in a dash of milk and carry my beverage to the lounge room. I ease myself into a seat and take a deep draught, the sweet tea sliding down my throat and warming my insides.

'Happy birthday,' I mutter to myself. At least it has been interesting, I ponder as I rise to my feet, my stomach growling as I realise I've missed dinner. I carry the empty cup and place it in the sink. I make a couple of fritz and sauce sandwiches, and as I munch on a half absentmindedly, I draw open the curtain and peer outside, looking for danger. I rub my shoulders as I feel suddenly chilled, and meander down the hall towards the bathroom.

Putting in the plug, I turn the two big taps. Water gushes into the ivory, claw-footed tub and steam soon fogs up the mirror. I strip off my garments and dip a foot into the steaming water, taking a sharp breath as the scalding water caresses my toes. I twist the hot water tap to off and cooling water continues to pour into the bath. As I wait, I brush my teeth and freeze. An eerie moan seems to creep up the pipes and echo out through the drain. Toothpaste foams out the side of my mouth as I glance down.

A finger pushes out of the drain cover and explores the sink, as if searching for something. I back away and cry out as I fall in the tub, water plunges over the side. Mortified, I scrabble at the tiles and pull myself up into a sitting position as a detached, decaying arm forces itself up through the pipes, slithers over the sink and lands on the floor. It crawls towards me, using its fingers as makeshift legs. The apparition slips and slides in the water and crashes into the side of the bath. I scream, leap out of the tub and pull the door shut behind me as I rush to my bed and dive under the covers, wet, aching and shaking.

This isn't real, pull yourself together. I laugh at the ridiculousness and the impossibility of a disembodied hand crawling up my plumbing. I giggle suddenly at the naughty innuendo. Even I'm not that deranged or desperate. I slip out of bed, my feet sinking into the plush shag on the floor, and I hurry through my bedroom doorway. Water seeps under the bathroom door and I take a deep breath, puffing out my chest in fake bravery. My fingers tremble as I turn the handle and thrust the door away from me. Like a cat ready to pounce, the arm is hunched in the corner. I take a step towards the bath; it turns as if sensing my presence and launches itself towards me. I halt and it stops.

I squash the desire to run screaming naked from my house, and inch on my tiptoes back against the wall, as if keeping the majority of my feet off the floor will deter it. I scream as it hurries towards me and I scramble into the tub and twist the cold water tap to the stop position. I shiver as I plunge into knee deep, tepid water. The disgusting limb hauls itself up a towel as I climb out of the bath. Frustration rushes through me. I grit my teeth; hot angry tears slide down my cheeks as I push open the bathroom window, wrap the insidious limb in the towel and fling it outside.

I take a heaving breath as I shut the window and hurry from the bathroom, taking my wet clothes from the floor and shoving them into the linen basket, but not before I plunge my hand into the jeans pocket and fish out a damp piece of paper. I choke back a sob as I realise the last number is illegible.

I take a towel from the linen press and dry myself. As I hurry to my bedroom to dress, I realise there is a very honest truth to the saying there is safety in numbers. As I stuff my feet into sneakers I almost sprint into the hall. I grab the white pages and my fingers tremble as I realise I don't know Gavin's last name; the white pages won't be useful in finding his number without it. I throw the book against the wall, my meek nature peeling away as if it was a second skin as I take on the painstaking process of entering the number nine times, using a different numeral for the final number each time.

'Hello,' a trembling female voice answers.

A human voice, thank goodness. 'Hello . . .'

'Please help me,' says the woman on the other end. 'I got bit and my leg's gone green.'

My voice is shaky as I reply. 'I'm sorry wrong number.' I hang up ready to make a new call. Several growls, moans and screams later, a familiar voice causes my cheeks to warm. 'Alara?'

'How did you know?' I manage to push out as my tongue suddenly feels heavy.

'Not many sheilas call me. Are you okay?'

'No,' I cry.

'I'm coming now. Stay inside.' The line clicks and I slide down against the wall and hug my knees to myself, my false bravado deflated.

Chapter Four

Unlikely Hero

As the loud vehicle meanders into my driveway and pulls up with the headlights off, a car door closes quietly. Heavy boots thud up my driveway and stop outside. As the flimsy screen is pulled open with a whining creak, a gentle rapping indicates my mulletted knight has arrived, willing to whisk me to safety.

I pull open the heavy wooden door and slip out, a backpack hoisted over my shoulder containing the most precious items I own: a photo album, my purse, a stuffed kangaroo from my childhood, a wad of cash—my entire life savings—amounting to two hundred and fifty dollars, six books and my library card. I'm not fickle and I know I am in a precarious situation; a knife and the contents of my food cupboard sits atop my precious lingerie. My mother's words echo in the back of my mind: "Don't forget to change your undies, you never know what may happen." and "A supportive bra is the best friend a woman can have."

I half-run half-walk to the vehicle, my dignity of little importance as I pull open the door and clamber inside, pulling it shut behind me. Gavin walks to my front door and secures it, before he hurries back to his car, and climbs in. With a roar the vehicle comes to life, and he turns towards me, a broad smile plastered across his face.

'I'm glad you are okay.' Gavin closes his door and plants his big hands on the steering wall as he shifts into reverse and pulls out of the driveway. As the vehicle gathers speed, he turns up the radio.

'Grrrr, this is brainy.' There is an awful moan. 'Radio, as per request, please enjoy juicy brains. I mean the 1964 smash hit, The Monster . . . grrrrr . . . juicy tasty brains.'

As the catchy refrains play something slams into the windscreen. The vehicle swerves as the tyres squeal on the bitumen. Gavin slams his feet on the brakes. I am catapulted forward and lose consciousness, a dull thud ringing in my ears as my head makes contact with the dash.

A sharp pain, scrapes the inside of my skull, forcing my eyes to open, my tongue is dry and a dull groan exits my mouth as I blink rapidly and focus in front of me. I am lying face down on the road. Blood trickles down my forehead and on to the ground as I force my hands, covered in gravel rash, on to the bitumen and push myself to my feet. I turn; my mouth hangs agape as I stare at the wreckage in front of me. The windscreen is shattered, a huge hole where I must have been flung forwards. I rub my arms, aware of how close they came to being shredded.

Oh crap, Gavin. I wince and shamble around to the driver's side as a zombie kangaroo twitches in the road. Its fur an emerald green, the swollen tongue lolls to the side as its eyes bulge, now a strange mustard yellow. I turn my head away as bile makes its way up from my roiling gut, burning my throat on its passage out of my body.

'Poor thing,' I mutter once the retching has stopped .

I wrench open the door; my hands sting and I make a sharp sound at the sudden pain. Gavin groans, and his eyes flutter open; his hands tremble on the steering wheel.

'You okay, love?' he asks.

I give him a warm smile. 'Sure.'

He laughs. 'You're a tough bird. You know that, right?'

I shrug and stare down at his legs. The car seems to have shrunken in size, the steering wheel has inched closer to his torso and his legs are crushed in by warped metal.

'I'm stuck.' He takes a trembling hand and points to the road in front. 'The farm is half an hour that way. Take a left down a semi-hidden track; the mailbox with thirteen on it will give it away. Get going and you will be safe.'

I roll my eyes and can't but help grin at his attempt at chivalry. 'Nah, we will do this together.'

Gavin groans as he tries to pull a leg out. 'I'm crushed in. We need something to use as leverage.'

I nod and hurry off to the side of the bitumen. Dark shapes line the eerie road and I can't see anything. Light suddenly floods the area. He is so thoughtful to turn on the headlights, I ponder as I scramble about looking for a heavy stick. Please let there be no zombie snakes. My investigation yields a large stick. I rush over to my new friend as a wave of dizziness threatens to uproot me from my upright position.

I slide the stick in between Gavin's legs. Leaning over, and with a downward thrust, I try to muster all my strength; metal creaks but barely budges. I turn my head to stare at my friend, his cheeks are bright red. He glances down at my chest, his eyes inch up to meet mine before he grins and looks away.

'I can't do this on my own.' I draw away.

'Too right. I'm firmly wedged in.' He grips the shaft in between his legs, his large, calloused hands gripped around its girth and I swallow hard. Don't be naughty, don't be naughty. This isn't the time for you to allow your loneliness to overcome your good sense. I need to swear off those romance novels.

'Help me, Alara. I can't handle this load on my own.'

I laugh suddenly. 'Oh, my gawd.'

'What did I say?' Gavin asks innocently.

I shrug and lean forward as a hand briefly brushes mine. We push downwards and metal squeals. Gavin draws a leg out as the stick snaps; his scream almost shatters me as the metal slams down on the remaining leg.

A tear slides down his face and he caresses my cheek with a warm hand. 'Go, love, I'll wait 'til help comes.

'Pfft.' I hurry around to the passenger side and grab my bag. I rummage around for the tomes then scurry around to his side. 'We will try this again. As we lift the metal off, we wedge in these books, giving us time before it comes crashing down on you again.'

He smiles sadly as if my suggestion is a foolish one. As he pushes down with all his might, sweat beads on his brow and his lip almost trembles as I notice the pain in his eyes.

'Hurry,' he mutters.

I wedge in the books as the shortened stick snaps again, its sound so loud in the tense dark it's like a gun going off right near me and I jump. Gavin groans and pulls the other leg out.

'Woohoo,' I cry and pump my fist in the air.

He uses the door to pull himself up, his body pressed up against mine. 'Thanks, love,' he mutters as he leans in and presses a sweet kiss to my cheek.' He groans as blood seeps through his ripped black jeans. 'I need to lean on you to get home. I'm sorry, mate.'

'Of course.' I square my shoulders as his mass crushes into me as I lean in under his arm, his arm wrapped around my side.

'Wait,' Gavin mutters as he leans down and grabs something sitting on the dash. 'Can't forget my lucky hat.' He places the black Akubra on his head and grins. 'Nonsense and superstition and all that jazz, I reckon. But I thought zombies weren't true blue before today as well.' He grins.

We painstakingly make our way past the zombie roo and Gavin halts. 'Can't leave the poor devil like that.'

I frown. 'Your good heart will get you killed,' I mutter.

We stumble forwards as the roo lifts itself to its feet and bounds away from us, its head at an odd angle. I shift us towards the passenger side and retrieve my bag and shoulder it before we amble down the road towards Gavin's farm.

Chapter Five

There is gold on the back of sheep

Gavin sags with exhaustion as we enter our sixth gate. Gloomy masses huddle against each other as the cloud cover recedes and the moon greets us like an ancient friend. Gentle bleating causes me to relax slightly as a sheep lifts its head in greeting, its soft amber eyes oblivious to the end of their world as they know it.

I shift my weight; Gavin groans and his body almost crushes me as he falls down with a thud in the paddock. A sudden cold gust of air howls around my ears and surges through the ankle-high grass, as if some fish was gliding its way through the vegetation that grows amongst the marshlands.

'Alara,' Gavin whispers.

I hunch down beside him and pat his arm, guilt streaks through me as I realise I was so distracted and didn't attend him straight away. 'Do you need to rest a bit?' I ask.

Gavin lifts his left leg, blood drips out from the left leg opening. I try to roll it up but the tight-fitting jean is snug against the muscled limb.

'Rip it,' he mutters.

I nod and stick my finger in a small distressed tear. Well, I'll add to the decoration. I give my friend a warm smile and tear; the garment rips easily and I spot the large, seeping gash. Shards of metal are imbedded in the muscle around the wound.

'Oh.' I cry.

Gavin sighs. 'Didn't want to bother you with it.'

I glare at Gavin. 'Men.' I rummage through my bag and blush as I look for something to stem the bleeding. I withdraw my bra and undies; Gavin winks and wolf whistles.

I roll my eyes and stare at the stuffed kangaroo. That stuffing would be ideal but I glance to the sheep as I rise to my feet and sprint towards the animals. The creatures scatter, bleating in distress as I chase them around the paddock in a futile attempt to harvest their wool.

Tears welling in my eyes, I rush towards Gavin, noting he has sat up and started pulling the shrapnel from his wound with a guttural cry I would love to hear between my sheets. I pull open the childhood toy, snatch up the stuffing and kneel before the wounded man, stemming the bleeding with the toy's insides as I bawl openly before this man, my dignity and self-control disappearing.

'I need something . . . to bind . . . it . . .' My words are interlaced with ridiculous sobs. I reach for my bra and tie it about the wound; it really is a great friend for situations like this.

'Was that important to you?' he asks.

I wipe my tears with the back of my hand. 'Uh ha.'

'Oh, I am so sorry.' Gavin gives me a sad smile.

A gentle bleating comes from behind me, and I turn as a sheep wanders over to the kindly farmer who holds out a tuft of grass. 'I made my money off these girls. There is gold on the back of sheep.'

'You could have called it over?' I ask, crossing my arms.

Gavin nods. 'Sorry, love, I was kind of in a bother.' He wipes his hand on his shirt and takes a knife from his pocket and slices off some wool. He snatches up the stuffed roo and pushes the new stuffing inside before he hands it back to me. 'I'll make it up to you and sew it up when we reach the house.' His kind smile warms me, but what he says next causes heat to spread all throughout my body.

'Good girl.' He pats the ewe, his tone almost husky, as if holding back tears.

'I wish you would say that to me,' I blurt out. Eeek. I rise to my feet and hurry a short distance away as Gavin's laughter shatters the air, my cheeks burning with indignation.

'You are a strange one,' Gavin shouts, 'but I need your help to get up.'

I trudge back towards him, my head held high, my mouth set in a thin line of determination. I stand next to him as he hoists himself up.

'Thanks,' he says.

I glance up and my eyes widen as he leans in and presses a questing kiss on my mouth, as if seeking permission. He draws away as if it never happened. 'You are a strange sort. But so am I.' He smiles and points towards the homestead with the large wrap around veranda looming ahead of us. 'Let's go.'

I run a finger over my lips as we make our way towards his home. Surely there would have been more to it than that. The security lights turn on and he pushes open the door. As I step over the threshold, he pulls me to his waist, tilts my chin upwards and stares at my mouth before he licks his lips; my knees threaten to buckle. As if waiting for my move, his eyes lock on mine. 'If I kiss you proper I reckon that'd make you my girl, wouldn't it?'

I nod and his mouth crashes down on mine, my mouth parting from the pressure. Our breath mingles, hot and wet, and I close my eyes as his hand grips mine and holds it against the door frame. He pulls away, his eyes full of something I am unsure of but yearn to explore.

'That was grouse.' He smiles. 'What's your last name, love?'

'Anderson,' I answer.

'Nice to meet you, Alara Anderson.' He absurdly holds out a hand to be shook, almost ridiculous after what we just shared. 'I'm Gavin Smith.'

I shake his hand and we both laugh nervously.

'Well, I'll show you to the spare room after I've tended to your head.' He enters the house and I follow.

Chapter Six

I've opened a can of worms.

The static of the radio buzzes in my ears as I turn the dial trying to find any AM frequency. Gavin is hard at work calling all his farmer mates, shearers and even his stockman. No one picks up and he stops flicking through his rolodex.

'Any one you need to call?' he asks.

I clench my jaw. I really should call her, my busybody grandmother, my only living relative after my parents died in a skydiving accident. They were fun, wild and outgoing, and after their death I was sent to live with my over-cautious grandmother, Ermintrude, who everyone called Trudy and I was no exception. My Nanna was strict and everything I did was never good enough. I sigh and make the call.

'Hello,' answers a cold voice. 'Best not be any more funny green men.'

'Trudy. It's me, Alara.' I wait.

'Oh, finally checking in on me after weeks. Typical,' she says and I can hear the disappointment in her voice. 'Did you put those green men up to knocking on the door and biting me as I opened it?'

'When did that happen?' I rasp out the astonished question.

'Late yesterday morning.' She coughs. 'Like, around ten am.'

My grandmother lives in the large town west of here, a few hours away. I risk a question I hope isn't confirmed. 'Are there lots of green people?' I ask.

'I'm going quite batty. I swear they're all over the place and even the animals are strange hues of green. The green people are on the telly too. You better not think I've gone crazy and send me away, Alara,' my grandmother rattles off.

I tense as I hear a loud bang on the other end of the line. My grandmother screams and I hear her cursing. 'Get away from me, you lousy bugger. Brains . . . what, get some of your own, ahh.' Then a loud growl followed by a whack and a thud before my hearty nanna gets back on the line. 'I dealt with her. Alice, my neighbour, took a chunk out of my ear. I got her good and proper. Wacked her with a potted plant, but she's lying on my favourite rug though.'

'Nan, I'm going to come get you,' I rush down the line.

My Nan laughs, a sound I rarely heard. 'Don't be silly, girl. I'm done for, but you know I was young when I had your mum. . . . grrr . . . and I wasn't firm with her. I tried to do right by you . . . I love you, girl . . . big brains and all.'

'Nan, wait,' I cry.

Gavin hurries over to my side. 'What's up, love?'

My Nan's next few words are what I waited all my life to here. 'I'm proud of you, kid.' Her voice is suddenly warm, like a smile in the dead of winter. 'Don't come, it's too late. Live your life.'

The line goes dead and I drop the receiver. It hangs by a cord and slaps gently against the wall. 'Well, that opened up a whole can of worms I didn't need to deal with right now as the world falls apart around us,' I cry out.

Gavin brushes the hair out of my eyes, his fingers touching the large adhesive dressing over the small cut on my head. 'We can try and get down there.'

'How?' I ask.

'Tractor or horse,' he answers.

'That'd be really stupid,' I mutter. 'We would probably die.'

Gavin shrugs. 'They will eventually come here too.'

'That's true.' I sigh. 'They would eat the horse.'

'It's your Nan. We have to go.' Gavin smiles. 'Family is everything.'

'Do you have any family?' I ask.

He takes a sharp breath and walks away from me, snatching up a picture frame nearby before handing it over. A smiling woman stands beside a man, a young child in her arms. The man appears to be Gavin a few years younger, he stares down at the woman and child, pure love shining out of his gorgeous eyes.

'Eight years ago.' Gavin frowns. 'My wife Kelley was a researcher in a bio lab, engineering cures for childhood illnesses. You see our girl Kylie was suffering from funny bouts of illness, slowly wasting away, and Kelley thought she could fix her. Her boss insisted that my wife test any potential cure on herself first. I expressed my concerns, but my wife was desperate to save our girl.'

Gavin stares down at the picture and frowns. 'When there were no side effects, she tried her cures on my girl. The bouts of illness stopped and my child seemed to be slowly recovering but then my wife became aggressive, even biting our child.' Gavin shudders. 'I had to keep her locked in the shed and called out the doctor. The company my wife worked for intercepted the call and sent their own doctor. I foolishly believed them when they said she was suffering from a virus and she would be fine. My girls both died a week later, a green sheen to their skin.' Gavin wraps his arms around me and squeezes the air from my lungs.

'You need to look out for family no matter how estranged you are. The company paid for the funeral and cremated their remains.'

Gavin releases me.

'I am so sorry that happened,' I rush out. My body fills with horror. I tremble. They may have been alive when that happened.

As if reading my thoughts, Gavin shakes his head. 'I was held down by the police when the company insisted on injecting the bodies with a serum and handed over a large wad of cash. Apparently, my wife signed a waiver when joining the research team that all evidence must be destroyed if a breakout occurs. I was escorted from the premises with a threat on my life if I blabbed. On the news the next day the business was destroyed in a convenient fire.'

I gawk at him, disbelief making my eyes widen.

He gives me a toothy grin. 'That was a lot to put on you.'

I shrug. 'I'm enjoying getting to know you.'

Gavin laughs. 'Well, not much else, I'm an old bugger, forty-two. I'm a Sagittarius, born December 1st. I like sheep and cows. I'm not one for veggies and my favourite colour is blue. I like talking to people but I also like my alone time.'

'Thanks for telling me all that at once.' I smile.

'Well, we will be travelling together to meet your Nan. Can't have her thinking you don't know me,' he says.

'Hmmm. I'm thirty-three, Scorpio, born October 31st. What a great last birthday that was. I'm a bookworm and librarian. I like my veggies and my favourite colour was green.' I shudder. 'Until recently.'

'Well, happy birthday, then.' Gavin pulls a five dollar note from his wallet. 'My dad always used to give me five bucks on my birthday, until he died twelve years ago. I continued that tradition with my family.' He hands me the note.

'Thank you,' I utter, touched by this simple and meaningful tradition that he is willing to share with me so openly.

'Have you ever been married?' he asks.

'No.' I mutter and glance away. 'Never even had a real date or boyfriend.'

'So, that was your first pash?' he asks.

I nod.

'Well, I'm supposed to say sorry for putting that on you. But I'd be lying if I wasn't a bit chuffed I was your first real snog.' Gavin runs a hand through my hair. 'I'll go get the tractor out. You go to the shed and get some supplies.'

He hurries away and I head to the back door, having been shown around briefly last night; the shed is next to the outhouse from what I recall. I hurry past the outside dunny and into the small shed. I glance around at the mismatched items—tools, a few old tins, a rifle—this is what he must mean by supplies. I push an old can aside as I grab the gun and pocket a few stray bullets. Something slithers out of a hole in the tin. I stare at the label: Cure Eight, Regrowth Serum Digitus.

A green caterpillar pops its head out, the black tip almost resembling a fingernail. Ha, a can of worms. I really have opened one; a possible boyfriend and a rescue mission during a zombie apocalypse to rescue my estranged Nan. I poke a dent in the can, five caterpillars stick out of various holes and clench and unclench in unison. My stomach jolts akin to the butterflies a caterpillar would become one day. But these little blighters were not such an insect but digitus—Latin for finger.

'Gavin,' I holler as I run towards the dull roar of an engine.

Gavin startles as I rush towards him, gun in hands. 'What is it?'

'The zombies started here.' I stop and gesture towards the shed. 'Those serums.'

My potential boyfriend pales and rubs his jaw. 'How can you be sure?'

'Green skin, biting and aggression. Your family was inflicted by it,' I rush out.

'Did the serum have a number?' Gavin asks, his voice shaky.

'Eight,' I answer.

He takes a deep breath. 'Her boss's serum. The ones her employer insisted on her testing. My wife's serums were all labelled with letters, and she never used the numbered serums on our child.'

'Oh gawd. What if it spreads through direct contact and not just bites?' I cry out.

'I have to make this right.' Gavin opens the tractor door and I take a sharp breath as I am lifted into his strong arms and hoisted up into the cabin. 'Scoot over.'

As I shuffle over, he squeezes himself in next to me, reaches over and takes the gun from my grasp and places it behind his seat. 'Ever handled one?' he asks.

I shake my head. 'No.'

'Right. Best I use it then.' He begins to drive and we fall into a comfortable silence.

Chapter Seven

It belongs in a romance novel

The hours pass slowly as we reach the outskirts of the large town. The end of the journey is an amalgamation of chaos, wrecked cars, bodies scattered on the road—both animal and human—shattered windows and roving packs of green-skinned citizens on the lookout for a feast. Small fires burn unchecked, and I hear screams as we slow down and turn into my Nan's street.

I point to the block of flats in the rougher part of town. 'Over there. At the end of the street.'

'Oh, I see the zombies have already played havoc here,' Gavin says, his gaze taking in the scene: burnt-out cars, overflowing bins, graffiti, couches thrown under the veranda to sit in and smoke, lone dogs roaming in the street.

I laugh loudly at his pure innocence or his overt attempt to be polite. He turns in his seat and smiles at me.

'What's so funny?' he asks, his face a mask of pure innocence.

'Nan lives in the poorer part of town. Her pension was barely enough to keep us kept,' I say.

Gavin frowns. 'I'm sorry, love, I didn't mean any offence. I bet as soon as you moved away you kept your Nan.'

I nod. 'Yeah, I send her money regularly.'

'Good girl,' he mutters and I melt within as he brushes my lips with his own.

He pulls away, grabs the gun and shoves open the door. I reach into my pocket and pass him the three bullets and he loads the weapon. Stepping down out of the cabin, he leans the gun against the huge tyre and holds up his arms. I lower myself into them and he places me on my feet.

We move quickly towards my Gran's door; a curtain is drawn aside and someone waves at us. We duck behind a car as a green-furred Pomeranian barks and scurries past, chasing a bird, its yaps fading into the distance. The sun looms above us and I glance down at my watch, twelve.

As we hurry towards the front of the house, the door is pulled open silently. A teenage girl hurries out of the house followed by a bunch of her peers all dressed in high school uniforms and armed with a medley of makeshift weapons.

'Rad. Good to not see some undead oldies,' says an older youth.

'How are a bunch of kids still alive?' asks Gavin.

The teenage girl who opened the door answers. 'All those between thirteen and eighteen seem unaffected.'

'That's not true. We passed a gang of zombie youths about fifteen minutes ago,' I say.

'As if,' says another kid.

I shrug. 'It's true. Have you been inside this whole time?'

The girl and her cohorts nod collectively as if in a state of shock.

'Well, I believe it's spreading through touch. Get inside and maybe you will stay safe,' I say and push past, heading to my Nan's house.

I glance back as the kids hurry inside and slam the door.

The doors to the pub across the street open and a mob of drunken zombies ambles unevenly all over the road towards us. Gavin aims his gun and fires; a hole opens up in the middle of a zombie, it stares down at the gaping wound and passes its hand through the gap.

'Grody,' it mutters as it slumps to the ground.

I slip the knife from my pocket and began slicing at the undead as they shuffle towards us, their voices becoming one long-winded groan as they mutter about brains. Gavin fires twice more and then begins swinging the gun like a club. The pile of undead grows and, as our assailants are defeated, we sprint down the road to my Nan's house.

I knock on Nan's door; slow, dull footsteps approach and an eerie drawn-out moan accompanies the person's approach. Gavin brushes me aside suddenly as the door is pulled aside. Nan, her pallor a vibrant fluorescent green, rushes the man I have deemed my future husband, her mouth wide open as she crashes into him, her teeth latched on to his forearm.

Chapter Eight

One Year Later

The radio on my desk splutters to life and I sigh and glance at the library doors. I have rigged up a complicated pulley system and my hand brushes the rope tied under my desk which I can untie if a relapse threatens my sanctuary.

'Welcome to the four pm news. The recovery is going well as the government continues to bring in brains to keep the inflicted well fed and almost their former selves as we continue to work on a cure. We encourage all the unafflicted to continue in their daily activities and do not discriminate against the inflicted as we know this disease only spreads through bites. We recommend the unafflicted take the necessary precautions to protect themselves in case a loved one relapses and tries to take a bite out of them. Remember, we are all in this together.'

The radio goes silent and I glance over to the teenagers we rescued doing their homework at the desks or lounging in bean bags talking quietly or reading books of interest. A green-skinned hand reaches up from behind me and places a library card on the desk.

'I found it in my purse.' My Nan stands up from her stooped rummage in her handbag as I check out her books.

She returned with us to town a year ago and we have started to overcome our past, despite her being a ravenous zombie. As the clock chimes, the teenagers wave to me and follow my Nan outside. I lock the door and hurry down the romance aisle, a broad grin plastered on my face.

Gavin, turns and smiles as he finishes stocking the returns. My grandmother's false teeth were unable to wound him and, like me, he is unafflicted. He grabs me in his arms, and he kisses me, my dear boyfriend.

'Strewth, I love you. Happy birthday, my love,' he mutters against my mouth.

Thirty-four and I've been kissed.